Little Red Conquers Her Fear of Flying

written by:
Tandy and Makenzie Schaller

This title is also available as a Tate Out Loud product. Visit www.tatepublishing.com for more information.

Published by Tate Publishing & Enterprises, LLC
127 E. Trade Center Terrace | Mustang, Oklahoma 73064 USA
1.888.361.9473 | www.tatepublishing.com

Tate Publishing is committed to excellence in the publishing industry. The company reflects the philosophy established by the founders, based on Psalm 68:11,
"The Lord gave the word and great was the company of those who published it."

Cover and interior design by Rhezette Fiel
Illustrations by Michael Roque

Published in the United States of America

ISBN: 978-1-62510-546-2
1. Juvenile Fiction / Action & Adventure / General
2. Juvenile Fiction / General
13.12.12

Dedication

We would like to dedicate this book to our former, present, and future students for inspiring and challenging our creativity.

In memory of Dorothy Latta—our mother, grandmother, and devoted Christian to all.

Acknowledgements

We would like to thank the following people, who have helped us in some way along our journey:

Our colleagues and friends for showing us that everyone has fears, and everyone can overcome them. Our family for enthusiastically supporting our dreams and believing in us.

Ken Schaller, Connor Schaller, and Donita Rachell for listening to our ideas and motivating us to share our creativity with others.

Preface

Once upon a time, there was a little girl who had many fears to overcome, just as most children do. This is the story of how Little Red conquered her fear of flying, with the help of her loving family.

But before we hear Little Red's story, you should know how Little Red got her name.

Now, Little Red wasn't just your ordinary nine-year-old girl. She earned her name justly, as her mother was Irish and her father was Scottish. Therefore, Little Red was born with a head of red, curly hair, and petite and spunky she was!

It seemed to her family as if Little Red would not be afraid of anything at all, but she most certainly was!

On this particular day, Little Red was lying in her warm, cozy bed, fretting about her upcoming family vacation. She had not traveled in a very long time and was not eager to do so any time soon. It wasn't that Little Red didn't like to travel. She really did want to discover new places with her family. But you see, the last time she had traveled, Little Red had gone to visit her grandmother, and it was a **horrifying** experience...

FLORIDA

Little Red's family woke up very early in the morning to catch a six o'clock flight to Florida. They lugged their many suitcases into the airport and made their way to the check-in counter.

Not wanting her family to know that she wasn't so sure about this vacation, Little Red kept her uneasiness to herself. She and her family made their way through the hubbub of the crowded airport to find the gate where they would board their plane. As her family waited, Little Red tried to keep her mind off of her fear of traveling by reading her new mystery book that she had bought at the book fair. Brother played games on Father's laptop and Little Red's parents talked about their plans for the vacation.

Finally, the time arrived to board the plane. Little Red's stomach was full of butterflies, but when the airline attendant called their seat numbers, she followed her parents to the gate. They stood in line like they were waiting to ride a roller coaster at an amusement park. Little Red thought that she would much rather be doing that. In her mind, Little Red was saying, *I can do this, I can do this*. As the passengers loaded the plane, she was surprised to see how calm everyone was.

All of the passengers had to walk through a long, narrow tunnel that led them to the plane. They were met by two smiling flight attendants. *These attendants seem* ***overly*** *friendly*, thought Little Red, who was still uncertain about the flight. The flight attendants gave Little Red and Brother a pair of plastic wings as a souvenir of the flight. Little Red looked suspiciously at the flight attendants as she stuck the wings to her shirt.

Little Red was amazed by how long the main aisle of the plane was and how many seats were on the plane. *Oh no,* she thought as she began to feel those butterflies fluttering in her stomach again. *How will this plane ever get off the ground with the weight of so many people on it?*

Little Red's worrying was interrupted by the sound of Father's voice saying, "Kids, here are our seats." He told them they would be sitting across the aisle from each other. Little Red would sit with Mother and Brother would sit with Father for the take-off. After that, she and Brother could sit together if they wanted to play a game. *Play a game? I can't even think about that!* Little Red just wanted to get through the take-off part!

Little Red watched as people continued to board the plane. When all of the seats were filled, she could hear the door of the plane slam shut and she knew that there was no getting off now. She realized that the saying "Make a beeline for the door" probably came from frightened people wanting to get off of planes.

Before she could dwell on this thought, Little Red heard a voice over the intercom system. It was the voice of the suspiciously friendly flight attendant instructing passengers to fasten their seat belts and to turn off all cell phones, computers, and Wi-Fi devices. Little Red thought this was odd, so she asked Mother about the announcement that the flight attendant had made. Mother told her that if passengers were to leave these electronics on, they could interfere with the pilot's controls and devices in the cockpit. *Wow,* thought Little Red, looking anxiously around the cabin, *I sure hope everyone turns them off!*

Before Little Red even had that horrifying thought out of her mind, she heard the flight attendant's voice again. This time she was talking and another smiling flight attendant was demonstrating how to use a breathing mask, "in case the cabin pressure should drop," the flight attendant told the passengers. *What is cabin pressure and why do we need a breathing mask if it drops?* Little Red wondered.

The flight attendant continued. Now she was explaining that their seat cushions could be used as a flotation device. Well if Little Red wasn't confused before, she certainly was now. *Why would I need a flotation device? Will we be flying over water? Do they really think this plane is going to crash? I don't even know how to swim!*

When the flight attendant finished talking, Little Red turned to her mother and said in a very anxious voice, "Mother, what does all that mean?"

Mother knew Little Red all too well and had anticipated her reaction. "Well," she began, "it is really nothing to worry about. You see, the airline wants passengers to be aware of what to do in an emergency, but these types of situations rarely occur."

"But they do happen sometimes?" asked Little Red.

"I guess they can happen, but remember what your father told you. Flying is safer than riding in a car."

Little Red did not feel consoled by that comparison, but she supposed it would have to do for now. Mother was getting ready to read her book and Little Red could tell that she did not want to be interrupted.

As the plane started moving, Little Red grasped the arm rests so hard that her knuckles turned a pale white. She looked out the window, watching as the plane picked up speed. She felt the front end lift off the ground, and then the back end. *We're in the air! The plane is flying!* Little Red watched the things on the ground get smaller and smaller. In just a few seconds, the cars and roads looked like Brother's little toy racetrack. The houses looked no bigger than the size of her fingernail. She couldn't believe how high they were going!

I hope we don't go much higher or we'll bump into the clouds.

Just as Little Red finished this thought, the view outside the window turned white. "Mother! What happened?"

"Those are clouds, Little Red; we are flying through the clouds."

How is that possible? Little Red wondered. Mother must have read her mind because she then said, "We can fly through clouds because they are made of gas, just like the air all around us, but clouds are white and the air around doesn't have a color."

Little Red remembered learning about gases in science. She couldn't wait to tell her teacher about clouds when she got back to school in a week. *If we survive this flight, that is!*

Little Red decided that she would try to get comfortable since they would be on the plane for a few hours. She got out her mystery book and began reading. Little Red was really getting into the mystery when she felt the plane lurch to the side. She froze.

What was that? Why did the plane do that? Did the pilot hit something? The plane lurched again. This time it felt like they hit a few things, as the plane jerked downward and from side to side.

Oh no! This must be what the flight attendant was talking about when she said a drop in cabin pressure! Why are the breathing masks not coming down from the ceiling? I can't breathe!

Mother looked up from her book and saw Little Red in a panic. "Dear, we just hit a few bumps in the clouds. We are going to be just fine. That happens to planes all the time."

"But Mother, what about the cabin pressure?" Little Red asked frantically.

"Oh, Little Red," her mother sighed, "there is nothing wrong with the cabin pressure. You just gave yourself a fright."

After hearing this, Little Red realized that she was breathing just fine. She guessed that she didn't need a breathing mask after all. She still felt uneasy, but tried to focus on her book.

Little Red read another paragraph, then the plane hit a bump again! This time, though, it didn't stop. The front end of the plane jerked downward and side to side as Little Red clenched the arm rests. Now she really felt like she was on a roller coaster, but this wasn't fun like the rides at an amusement park! She looked at her mother, who was still reading her book. *What is wrong with her? This plane is going to crash! I need my flotation device!*

Little Red unbuckled her seat, stood up, and tried to pull her seat cushion off like the flight attendant had instructed. She pulled and tugged on the cushion, but it wouldn't budge. She could feel the plane going down!

The flight attendant hurried down the aisle when she saw Little Red trying to detach the seat cushion. "May I ask what you are doing, little girl?" she said in an annoyed tone.

"I need my flotation device! Can't you feel the bumps? The plane is going to crash!" Little Red exclaimed.

Mother and the flight attendant looked at each other and chuckled. The flight attendant spoke calmly, "The bumps you felt were caused by the plane traveling back down through the clouds. We are preparing to land in Florida."

Mother then said, "Little Red, look out the window. We are about to land at the airport." Little Red looked out the tiny window and saw the roads, cars, and houses getting bigger. "You need to sit down now and buckle up for the landing," Mother told her.

As Little Red slowly turned around and sat down in her seat, she felt awfully silly. She had made a big scene on the plane for nothing. She felt the front wheels of the plane hit the runway, and then the back wheels. The plane slowed down and the pilot drove right up to the gate. "Welcome to Florida, the Sunshine State!" the flight attendant said in a cheerful voice over the intercom.

Whew! I am glad to be on the ground again!

Little Red thought about the flight as they exited the plane. *I guess that wasn't so bad. It was actually kind of fun flying up in the clouds, and it only took us a few hours to get to Florida. That sure beats a long car trip! Next time we fly I won't be scared.* Now Little Red could enjoy her vacation with her family and not worry about the flight home!

listen|imagine|view|experience

AUDIO BOOK DOWNLOAD INCLUDED WITH THIS BOOK!

In your hands you hold a complete digital entertainment package. In addition to the paper version, you receive a free download of the audio version of this book. Simply use the code listed below when visiting our website. Once downloaded to your computer, you can listen to the book through your computer's speakers, burn it to an audio CD or save the file to your portable music device (such as Apple's popular iPod) and listen on the go!

How to get your free audio book digital download:

1. Visit www.tatepublishing.com and click on the e|LIVE logo on the home page.
2. Enter the following coupon code: c266-2375-b208-c04e-b3f6-825e-e5e2-1e31
3. Download the audio book from your e|LIVE digital locker and begin enjoying your new digital entertainment package today!